CHICAGO PUBLIC LIBRARY

P9-CQJ-061

R00595 73589

X

JUV FIC Shulevitz, Uri, 1935-

The magician

Cop. 1

$9.95

DATE			

SOUTH SHORE BRANCH
2505 EAST 73rd STREET
CHICAGO, ILLINOIS 60649

© THE BAKER & TAYLOR CO.

Uri Shulevitz
The Magician

An adaptation from the Yiddish of I. L. Peretz

Macmillan Publishing Company
New York
COLLIER MACMILLAN PUBLISHERS

LONDON

Ju/
Fic
cop. 1

Adapted from *Der Kunzen-Macher (The Magician)* by I. L. Peretz
Copyright © 1973 by Uri Shulevitz
All rights reserved. No part of this book may be reproduced
or transmitted in any form or by any means, electronic or
mechanical, including photocopying, recording or by any
information storage and retrieval system, without
permission in writing from the Publisher.

Macmillan Publishing Company
866 Third Avenue, New York, N.Y. 10022
Collier Macmillan Canada, Inc.

First published 1973; reissued 1985
Printed in the United States of America

10   9   8   7   6   5   4   3   2   1

Library of Congress Cataloging in Publication Data

Shulevitz, Uri, date.
The magician : an adaptation from the Yiddish
of I.L. Peretz.

Originally published: New York : Macmillan, 1973.
Summary: An old couple with neither food nor candles
to celebrate Passover receive a mysterious visitor
who supplies everything they need.
[1. Passover—Fiction] I. Peretz, Isaac Leib,
1851 or 2-1915. Kuntsn-makher. II. Title.
PZ7.S5594Mag 1985   [E]   85-42955
ISBN 0-02-782770-4

To Helen and Joseph Tannenbaum

One day a magician came
to a small village.

He was traveling on foot.

"Where from?" the villagers asked.

"Far away," the stranger replied.

"Where to?" they wanted to know.

"The big city," he said.

"Then what are you doing here?" they asked.

"I lost my way," he replied.

He was an odd fellow.
He was ragged and tattered,
yet he wore a top hat.
He gathered people around him on the street.
One minute he was full of tricks
and the next, he disappeared.
Just like that.

He pulled ribbons out of his mouth
and turkeys out of his boots.

He whistled, and rolls and loaves of bread
danced through the air.
He whistled again.
Everything vanished!

He scratched his shoe
and there was a flood of gold coins.

Yet he looked poor and hungry.

It was the eve of Passover.

All the houses in the village were lighted up
and filled with the smell of festive cooking.

And on each table, set for the holiday feast,
there stood an extra goblet of wine.
It was Elijah's cup,
prepared for the prophet,
a hoped-for guest
in every household on this holiday.

Only one house, where there lived
a poor man and his wife, remained dark.
They had no food and not even a single candle.
Yet they would not ask for help.
"There are people who are worse off than we are,"
the old man said. "We will manage."

Night came.

"Happy holiday," the old man said to his wife.

"Happy holiday," she replied.

But she could not help adding:

"Passover is here and we still have nothing."

"The Maker of the Universe does not
abandon his creatures," the old man said.
"And if God does not want us to have our
own Passover feast, then we must bow
to his will and attend someone else's.
Come, we'll be welcome at our neighbor's."

At that moment
the door opened and a voice said,
"May I be your guest for Passover?"

"I'm sorry," the old man said.
"We are poor and have nothing to offer you."

"I have everything we need," the voice replied.

The visitor waved his hands
and two lighted candlesticks appeared.

The old couple recognized the magician.

He signaled again
and a beautiful cloth spread itself
over the table, which slid quietly
to the center of the room.

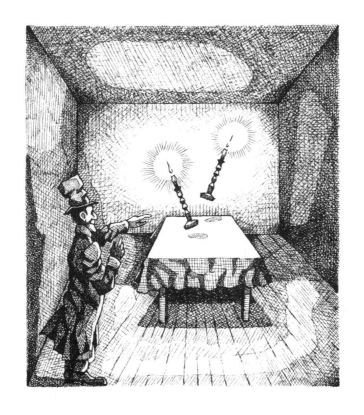

The candlesticks floated slowly down
to meet it and settled into place.

"Now we need chairs to sit on!"
the magician called out. The wooden benches
that had been standing against the walls
skimmed the floor and stopped at the table.

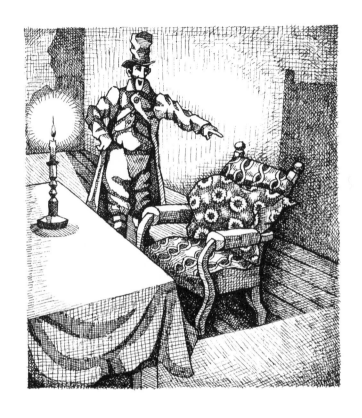

"Get soft," he ordered, and the benches
became armchairs with pillows as backrests.

Out of nowhere, one object after another,
everything that was needed to celebrate
the holiday appeared on the table.

The old couple could not believe
what they saw.

"There is good magic and evil magic," the old
man whispered to his wife. "We must not
touch anything. We must be sure that evil
is not at work here to tempt and deceive us.
Let us go and ask the rabbi's advice."
The old woman threw her shawl over her
head and they hurried to the rabbi's house.

When the rabbi heard their story, he said:
"Evil magic cannot create real things. It can
only fool the eyes. If you can taste the food
and pour the wine, if you can sit in the chairs,
then they are real and sent from heaven."

The old couple returned home
and found everything just as they had left it.
But the magician was gone.

They tasted the food,
they poured the wine into glasses.
They sat in the armchairs
among the soft pillows.
Everything was real.

Only then did they know
it was not a magician
but the prophet Elijah himself
who had visited them.